The HIDDEN LITERATURE

VAGISHA SINHA

ISBN
Paperback 979-8-89777-960-4
Hardcase 979-8-89984-567-3

Contents

Contents

Chapter 1

The Door Beneath the Library

Olivia loved books more than anything in the world. Every afternoon after school, she would rush to the town library, excited to get lost in another story. The library was her favorite place, an old building with wooden floors that creaked underfoot and shelves stacked high with books of every kind. The smell of paper and ink filled the air, making her feel safe, like she belonged among the pages of a thousand different adventures.

On this particular day, it was raining, tapping softly against the tall windows of the library. Most people had gone home, leaving the place quiet except for the occasional rustle of turning pages. Olivia wandered deeper into the library, searching for something new to read. She had already finished all her favorite books—twice.

As she ran her fingers along the dusty old books in the farthest corner, her hand suddenly brushed against something odd. The back of the bookshelf felt... hollow.

Shocked, Olivia came closer. That's when she noticed it— a small wooden door, barely visible behind the heavy bookshelf. Her heart skipped a beat. A secret door? She glanced around, expecting a librarian to appear and tell her she wasn't supposed to be there. But no one was watching.

Curiosity burned inside her. She reached out and pressed against the door. It creaked open easily, revealing a narrow, spiraling staircase leading downward into darkness. A cool, dusty smell drifted up, which sent shivers down her body.

Olivia hesitated. Should she go back? Should she tell someone?

But then she thought about all the books she had read, stories where heroes took risks and discovered hidden treasures. This was her moment. If she turned back now, she'd always wonder what was down there.

Taking a deep breath, she stepped inside.

The door swung shut behind her.

The staircase was old, and the stone steps were uneven beneath her feet. The deeper she went, the darker it became. She ran her fingers along the cold, damp wall to keep her balance. The only sound was her own breathing and the echo of her footsteps.

Then, after what felt like forever, she reached the bottom.

Before her stretched a vast underground chamber, much larger than she had expected. A giant chandelier hung from the ceiling, its candles flickering with a strange golden glow. Shadows danced across the stone walls, making the room feel almost alive. But what really caught her attention were the books.

Rows and rows of towering bookshelves lined the chamber, stretching far and beyond what her eyes could see. The books were old; some were covered in thick layers of dust, others looking as if they had never been touched at all. But that wasn't the strangest thing.

The books were whispering.

A soft whisper filled the air, like hundreds of voices speaking at once. It wasn't loud, but it was enough to make the hair on her arms stand up.

Olivia swallowed hard. Was she imagining this?

She took a cautious step forward. The whispers grew louder. Her eyes were looking around, but there was no one else in the room.

Slowly, she reached out and touched the back of a thick, leather-bound book. The moment her fingers brushed against it, the whispers stopped.

For a second, there was silence.

Then, a single voice, soft yet clear, whispered:

"Help us..."

Olivia pulled her hand away, her heart pounding.

The book had spoken.

She moved backward, breathing hard. She wanted to run back up the stairs, forgetting she had ever found this place. But she also wanted to stay and feel all the adventure.

Taking a breath, she looked around again. Her eyes landed on a book resting on a statue in the center of the room. It was different from the others, larger, with a cover of deep blue leather and gold lettering that glowed in the candlelight.

She stepped closer.

The title read:

"The Kingdom of Eldoria: An Unfinished Tale."

Olivia hesitated because something about this book felt important, as if it had been waiting for her.

Her fingers were around the book as she slowly opened the cover.

The moment she opened the cover, a golden light came from the pages, which wrapped around her like a warm embrace. The library around her blurred. She felt like her head was spinning.

Olivia gasped. And then, she was gone.

The Library of Forgotten Stories

Olivia felt like she was falling.

Wind passed through her, making her hair whip around her face. She tried to scream, but no sound came out of her mouth. Her stomach rolled over as she was trying to go through what felt like a swirling tunnel of golden light. The glow wrapped around her; it was warm and soft, like the pages of an old book come to life.

Then, just as suddenly as it began, it stopped.

She landed on her feet with a soft *noise*, but the ground beneath her wasn't stone or wood. It was smooth, almost silky. Blinking in surprise, Olivia looked down and gasped.

She was standing on a giant open book.

The pages stretched beneath her feet, covered in curling, inky letters that glowed. Around her, there were endless rows of bookshelves that reached high into the golden, misty sky, disappearing into the distance. The air smelled of ink and paper, but also something more magical—like the scent of rain just before it falls or the feeling of a dream going away when you wake up.

This wasn't the underground chamber anymore.

This was something far beyond that.

A deep, gentle voice broke the silence.

"Welcome, Olivia, to the Library of Forgotten Stories."

Olivia's face looked worried. Behind a grand wooden desk, there was a tall man standing with knowing eyes. His silver beard flowed down to his chest, and his robe shimmered with threads of gold and silver yarn, as if woven from the stories that were within them. His hands rested on an unknown, leather-bound book, its pages glowing softly.

Olivia's breath caught. "Who... who are you?"

The old man smiled, his eyes twinkling like candlelight. "I am the Keeper of Lost Tales," he said. "And you, young one, have found a place that few ever do."

Olivia turned around slowly, trying to think about what exactly was happening. Shelves upon shelves stretched endlessly in every direction; these shelves were stacked with books that had a golden light on them. Some were open, and their pages were moving as if caught in a breeze, while other books sat perfectly still and waiting.

"Where... am I?" she asked. She was still feeling dizzy.

The Keeper stepped forward. "This is where unfinished stories come to rest," he said. "Every book here holds a story that was started but never completed – a forgotten dream, a story that was left behind."

Olivia questioned, "Why are they here? Why didn't you let them fade away?"

The Keeper sighed; his expression grew sad after listening to her. "Because no story truly disappears, child. Even when a tale is forgotten, its words will always exist. These books wait, longing for someone to remember them… longing for an ending."

Olivia swallowed. The books seemed to shake, as if they were agreeing with his words.

She looked down at the book; it was still in her hands—the one she had picked up in the underground chamber. The golden title sparkled in the soft light:

"The Kingdom of Eldoria: An Unfinished Tale."

Her fingers tightened around the cover. "And this one?" she asked. "Why did it bring me here?"

The Keeper tried to study her for a long moment. Then he said, "Because the story inside is not finished. And it has chosen you to complete it."

Olivia's heartbeat increased. "Me?" she whispered. "But... I don't know how to finish a story!"

The Keeper's eyes sparkled. "Perhaps not yet. But the story will show you the way."

Olivia looked back at the book. Her hands tightly gripped the book. She had always loved reading stories—but writing them? Finishing them? That was something she had never imagined before.

"Can I really do this?" she wondered.

Before she could say anything else, the book in her hands began to glow.

The golden light sparkles around her, brighter and warmer than before. The Library of Forgotten Stories faded before her eyes.

The last thing she heard was the Keeper's voice, yet it was not that clear:

"Remember, young one... A story is only truly lost when no one is left to tell it."

Then, in a flash of gold, Olivia was gone.

Chapter 3

A Kingdom in Trouble

Olivia landed hard on the ground. She was rolling onto her side as the golden light faded around her. The air was different here. It smelled like earth and woodsmoke, with a faint hint of flowers carried on the breeze.

Groaning, she sat and blinked.

She was in the middle of a village, but it wasn't like a town she had ever seen before; something about that town felt different. Scratched roof cottages lined the streets, their wooden shutters were painted in bright blue and red. Stalls were set up on the side of the road, which had fresh bread, golden apples, and bunches of wildflowers.

People hurried through her. People over there were dressed in long coats and boots, their arms full of baskets. But something was wrong.

There was a feeling in the air – a nervousness, an unspoken fear. Even though the village should have been lively, there were no laughing children, no music, no friendly chatter; it almost felt like everybody was in depression. People walked quickly, rushing so much that many of them were just glancing over each other's shoulders as if expecting something terrible to happen at any moment.

Olivia's stomach tightened.

Where am I?

She slowly got to her feet, dusting herself off. Her hands were still holding the book—The Kingdom of Eldoria: An Unfinished Tale.

This must be Eldoria.

But why did it feel like a place waiting for disasters?

Olivia took a deep breath and approached an old man sitting on a wooden bench near the well. His clothes were faded, and his hands were rough like stone, as if he had spent a lifetime working. His eyes looked kind, and he was filled with worry.

"Excuse me," she said hesitantly. "Can you tell me where I am?"

The man turned to her slowly, as if he had only noticed her standing there. His eyes flicked to the book in her hands.

"You... You shouldn't be here," he whispered. His voice was deep and seemed to be tense. "If the Shadow King's men find you, they will take you away."

Olivia's heartbeat increased. "The Shadow King?" Who is he?

The man looked around nervously, lowering his voice. "You should leave, child. It seems like he is searching for something. Or someone."

Olivia's grip on the book tightened.

Before she could ask anything else, a deep horn sound rang out in the distance.

The villagers stopped.

A moment later, the sound of a horse running very fast echoed down the street.

Olivia turned to see the group of riders heading toward the village square, their horses kicking up dust. Their leader, a tall man with armor as dark as the night sky, pulled back his reins and held up a hand.

The villagers cowered all around.

"By order of the Shadow King," the man said, "we seek the girl with the book."

Olivia's breath caught in her throat. They were looking for her.

I need to run.

But before she could move, the old man beside her reached out and grabbed her arm. His eyes were frightened.

"Go," he whispered. "Find the Seeker. She is the only one who can help you."

Olivia hesitated for only a second. Then she clutched the book to her chest and ran away.

Chapter 4

The Chase Begins

Olivia's breath caught in her throat as a hand gripped her shoulder.

She turned around, her heart hammering in her chest. Her eyes struggled to adjust to the darkness, but she could make out a figure standing in the shadows, a tall person with a hood over their face.

'Shh,' the stranger whispered. 'They're right outside.'

Olivia's pulse raced.

Outside, the sound of animals walking and soldiers shouting echoed through the street.

"She must be here, somewhere around us!" a soldier said loudly. "You must check every house!" the soldier ordered.

Olivia was so scared. If they searched the houses one by one, it was only a matter of time before they found her.

The stranger seemed to sense her fear. "Follow me. Quickly."

Olivia hesitated. Could she trust this person? She didn't even know who they were. But she had no choice. If she stayed, she would be caught.

She nodded and said, "Okay," in a whispering voice.

The figure moved a little, which led her through the dark room. They searched between tall bookshelves and wooden desks covered in parchment; they went through the shadows as if they knew this place well.

Then, they stopped in front of a large bookshelf at the farthest end of the room. Without a word, the stranger pressed their palm against a hidden latch, and the bookshelf opened, revealing a narrow passageway.

Olivia's eyes widened. A secret tunnel?

"Go," the stranger requested.

Olivia stepped inside, and the stranger followed her. The stranger was pulling the bookshelf that shut behind them.

Darkness made Olivia more scared.

For a moment, there was only silence and peace, but the sounds of soldiers outside were growing louder and louder.

Then, the stranger lit a small lantern, but lights were still flickering across the stone walls of the tunnel.

"We should be safe here," they said.

Olivia finally could speak. "Who are you?"

The stranger pulled back their hood.

A boy, who was not older than fifteen, with messy dark hair and green eyes, stood before her. His clothes were torn, his boots were covered in dust, and a silver bag hung from his belt.

"My name is Kieran," he said. "And you just made yourself the most wanted person in Eldoria."

Olivia said, "I didn't mean to! I - I don't even know how I got here!"

Kieran studied her for a long moment; his eyes were only looking at the book that she clutched to her chest.

"That book," he said slowly. "Where did you get it?"

Olivia hesitated. Should she tell him the truth? Would he even believe her?

"I found it... in a library," she said carefully. "But not here. I found it in my world."

Kieran's eyes narrowed.

"Your world?"

Olivia nodded. "I don't know how, but when I opened this book, I was pulled into this place. And now the Shadow King's soldiers are after me because of this book."

Kieran's expressions darkened. "If they're after you, it's because of that book."

Olivia looked down at it. The golden letters on the cover shimmered in the dim lantern light.

"The Kingdom of Eldoria: An Unfinished Tale."

Kieran exhaled. "Then you really don't know, do you?"

"You know what?"

Kieran hesitated.

'That book doesn't just hold a story. It holds the destiny of this kingdom.'

Olivia said, "The destiny of Eldoria?" she repeated.

Kieran nodded. "The Shadow King has been searching for it for years. He believes that whoever owns it, that person will control the kingdom's future. But no one has ever found it."

He stepped closer.

"Until now."

Olivia's head was spinning. She had always loved books, always dreamed of adventure – but she had never imagined that she would become part of one.

"What does the Shadow King want to do with it?" she asked.

Kieran's jaw tightened. "He wants to rewrite the story. So that he can bend the kingdom's fate to his will. If he gets his hands on that book, Eldoria will be lost."

A chill ran down Olivia's body.

"So what do we do next?" she whispered.

Kieran's expression was stressed.

"We will run," he said. "And we will find the one person who might be able to stop him."

Olivia clutched the book tightly.

"Who?"

Kieran's green eyes shimmered in the lantern light.

"The Forgotten Queen."

Chapter 5

Secrets of the Forest

Olivia's legs were tired as she ran, struggling to follow Kieran. The narrow tunnel twisted and turned; the stone walls were very cold. Their lanterns barely lit the way, casting strange shadows that danced around them.

Behind them, the echoes of shouts and the sound of metal boots on stone sent shivers up Olivia.

"They're searching the whole town," Kieran whispered. "We don't have much time."

Olivia's chest tightened as she held the book closer. What was so special about it? Why was the Shadow King so desperate to find it?

Kieran stopped suddenly.

"We're close," he said.

Olivia became serious. "Close to what?"

Kieran turned to her, his green eyes serious.

"To the only way out of the city."

He pushed the tunnel wall, and with a soft click, a door opened, revealing the outside world.

Olivia gasped.

They both were standing at the edge of a dense and misty forest; the trees were stretching high above them. The city walls appeared in the distance; torches were flickering as soldiers searched for her.

Kieran grabbed her hand.

"Come on."

They tried to dart into the forest.

Olivia's heart pounded. The trees twisted and loomed over them, their rough branches reaching out like fingers. The air smelled earthy, but something else felt weird beneath the surface—something ancient, something watching.

Kieran slowed down, his eyes scanning the trees. "We have to be careful."

'Why?' Olivia whispered.

"The Eldorian Forest is alive," Kieran said. "It doesn't look like outsiders."

Olivia swallowed. "What do you mean, alive?"

Kieran didn't answer. Instead, he took a cautious step forward, his fingers brushed against the nearby tree. The moment he touched it, the tree shook.

Olivia gasped as the tree's bark rippled out, forming a strange pattern that almost looked like... a face.

The tree groaned loudly. A low, whispery voice echoed through the air.

"Travelers of fate... what is it you seek?"

Olivia stopped and asked, "Can the trees talk?"

Kieran nodded. "We are looking for the passage through the forest."

The whispering voices grew louder, moving through the leaves like a thousand unseen creatures.

"Among you, one carries the book of lost fate…"

Olivia tightened her grip on the book.

"The story must be completed… or the kingdom will fall."

The story… She had to finish the story?

The tree's face shifted, and the whispering faded. Then, the branches slowly parted, forming a clear path ahead.

Kieran grabbed Olivia's arm. "Let's go. Before they change their minds."

Olivia nodded quickly as her mind was racing.

She wasn't just inside a book.

She was part of a story that was waiting to be finished.

And if she failed, Eldoria would be lost forever.

Chapter 6

The Hidden Village

The path stretched before them, its winding trail was barely visible because of the thick mist. Olivia and Kieran moved slowly, their footsteps quiet on the earth. The trees around them whispered; their branches were shifting as if they were watching.

Olivia shivered. "How much further?"

Kieran looked quickly at the darkening sky. "Not far. But we have to hurry. The forest changes at night."

Olivia didn't like the sound of that. "Changes, how?"

Kieran's jaw tightened. "I mean that it's not friendly after dark."

As they walked further, the trees grew denser, their branches interwoven like a tangled web. Glowing mushrooms dotted the ground, casting a strange green light. Every now and then, Olivia thought she saw shadows moving beyond the trees, but whenever she turned, there was nothing there.

Finally, after so many hours, the trees thinned. A small wooden passage stood before them, covered in glowing blue flowers. Beyond it, there was a village unlike anything Olivia had ever seen spread out.

Houses were made out of woven branches that nestled against the trees, their windows glowing with warm candlelight.

Kieran took a relieved breath. "We made it."

Olivia asked, "What is this place?"

"The Hidden Village," Kieran said. "It's one of the last safe places in Eldoria. The Shadow King's forces can't enter here."

Olivia exhaled deeply, feeling a little safer. But inside, she knew that safety wouldn't last forever.

A woman stepped forward, her long silver hair shimmering in the dim light. Her eyes were kind, but they were filled with a deep wisdom that made Olivia feel small.

"Bring the book to me," the woman said softly. "Then the time has come."

Olivia's stomach tightened. "The time for what?"

The woman didn't answer. Instead, she turned back and gestured for them to follow her. Olivia exchanged a look with Kieran before stepping forward.

Whatever was happening, she had a feeling that her journey had just begun.

Chapter 7

A Mysterious Prophecy

Olivia followed the silver-haired woman through the village. She could feel that the villagers were only looking at her, their whispers rising like a soft voice through the narrow streets. Some of them looked at her in awe, others in fear, and a few with hope. She wasn't sure which reaction made her more nervous.

The woman took her to a massive tree at the heart of the village; its trunk was so thick that it would take at least ten people to encircle it. Its ancient branches stretched high into the sky, their golden leaves moving softly in the wind. A wooden door had been carved into the bark of the tree; it blended so seamlessly with the tree that it looked like part of the trunk itself.

"This way," the woman said, pushing the door.

Olivia hesitated for a moment before stepping inside.

The room was dimly lit by hundreds of tiny candles; they were flickering. The air was filled with the fragrance of dried herbs, parchment, and something metallic—like old coins or rusted iron. Shelves lined the walls; these walls were overflowing with scrolls and books. They were so ancient that their pages were crumbling at the edges. A wooden table was placed in the center; it was covered in maps, ink bottles, and strange symbols that were carved into small glowing stones.

The woman gestured for Olivia to sit. "I am Lady Evora, the Keeper of the Old Ways. And you... you are the one the prophecy spoke of."

Olivia's breath caught in her throat. "Prophecy?"

Evora nodded, her expression unreadable. She took a large scroll; its edges were cracked, and it was carefully unrolled across the table. The parchment was so delicate that it looked like it might crumble at the lightest touch. The ink faded in some places, but the words were still clear and strong, as they had been waiting for this moment.

Olivia leaned in, her eyes scanning the ancient script:

"When the Kingdom falls into shadow, a savior from the other world shall come, bearing the lost book. With ink and courage, they shall write the destiny of Eldoria. But only through their words shall the kingdom find its end—whether in ruin or rebirth."

"A savior of the other world... that means me, doesn't it?" she whispered.

Evora nodded. "Yes. You were not meant to find the Library of Forgotten Stories by accident. The book chose you, and you must decide the destiny of Eldoria."

Olivia has always loved stories, but she never imagined being inside one, especially one where the entire kingdom depended on her choices.

"But... I don't know how to finish the story," she said, her voice barely audible.

Evora studied her closely, then she took out another scroll; this one was new, with writing that looked different from the ancient script. She opened it and revealed illustrations of past heroes, magical creatures, and battles from the old times.

"You must learn," Evora said. "The Shadow King's power is growing stronger day by day. His army has already begun to find you. If you do not complete the story, he will rewrite it in his own image—and Eldoria will be lost."

"How... how do I do it?" she asked. She pretended like she is braver than anyone in this world.

Evora took out a small leather-bound book from her drawer and handed it to Olivia. The cover was blank, but when she touched it, words appeared on the first page:

"The Unwritten Story."

"This book," Evora explained, "will allow you to see the truth hidden behind Eldoria. It will reveal to you what has been forgotten, and this will help you guide your hand. But be cautious—what you write in it will actually happen. Words have power, Olivia. You must choose them wisely."

Olivia stared at the book, her fingers first moved around the smooth cover. Could she really do this? Could she truly change the destiny of an entire kingdom with just words?

A strong wind suddenly blew through the room, making the candles flicker. Evora's eyes darkened.

"The Shadow King's people are near," she said. "We do not have much time. You must go to the Cursed Tower before it is too late."

Olivia asked, "The Cursed Tower?"

Evora nodded. "It is the place where the Shadow King first gained his power, and this is the place where the last storyteller was lost. If you understand how to finish this story, you must uncover the truth hidden within its walls."

Olivia gripped the book tightly.

She had always dreamed of adventures, like being the hero she read about in books. But now, she faced the reality of her situation.

She wasn't just a reader anymore.

She was a writer and the person who would write the destiny of Eldoria.

Taking a deep breath, she looked Evora in the eye.

"I'll do it," she said.

Evora smiled; still, there was sadness in her expression. "Then may the words guide your path, young storyteller."

As Olivia stepped out of the tree and into the moonlit village, she knew one thing that she believed in, which was that this was no longer just a story.

This was her story.

And she had to finish it.

Chapter 8

The Cursed Tower

Olivia was standing at the edge of the forest. She was staring at the dark tower that caught her eye from a distance. It was taller than anything she had ever seen before; its black stone walls stretched toward the sky. The clouds above were in strange patterns.

Olivia shivered but took a deep breath and said, "This is the place where all the answers are," she said. "If we want to stop the Shadow King, we need to go inside."

The old woman in the village spoke about this tower in quiet tones. Legends claim that it was once a great castle and home to a powerful sorcerer. But after a terrible incident, the sorcerer cursed the tower. No one who entered had ever returned.

"We don't even know how to get in," Rylan said. "I think that the door has been locked with magic."

Olivia took the Book of Eldoria from her shoulder. She flipped through the pages, and she started searching for clues. The book had guided her before, but it would help again. As she turned a page, the letters began to glow and came in front of her eyes:

"The key is not made up of metal, but of heart. To enter, one must show their deepest truth."

Olivia read the words aloud. Finn scratched his head. "What does that mean?"

'It means that the tower will not let us enter unless and until we prove something to the tower.'

Olivia nodded as she stepped closer. She went and placed her hand on the cold metal. A deep, strange voice echoed through the air.

"Who dares to seek entrance to the Cursed Tower?"

Olivia swallowed hard but answered, "I am Olivia, and I seek the truth."

The voice came as if it were considering her words. Then the doors began to glow, and a symbol appeared: a mirror showing the faces of all three of them.

"It's... us," Finn said.

Olivia was staring at her reflection. But something was different and unusual about it. The girl in the mirror didn't look just like her; she looked afraid and unsure. The image flickered, as it was showing some moments of doubt from her past times when she wanted to give up and when she doubted herself.

The voice boomed again.

"To enter, you must face your fears."

Olivia said, "I... I don't know how."

"You do," Rylan said softly. "You've been facing them all the time."

Olivia took a deep breath. "I'm afraid of failing," she admitted, her voice shaking, but she did it. "I'm afraid that I won't be able to help this kingdom and I won't be strong enough to do this."

The mirror shone brightly, and suddenly, the reflection changed. Instead of doubt, she saw moments of courage and happiness standing up to the Shadow King's riders, who were helping the villagers, pushing forward even when she was scared.

"You are more than your fear," Rylan said.

With a deep breath, Olivia stepped forward. The doors of the tower opened and then, finally, the door opened.

Cold air rushed through as they stepped in. The room was dimly lit, with a spiraling staircase winding upward. Strange symbols glowed on the walls. In the center of the room, an ancient throne was kept, which was covered in dust.

"This place is... strange," Finn whispered.

Olivia walked toward the throne. She was a little nervous about it, but she did it. As she reached out, the book in her hands began to glow.

"You have entered my tower," the figure said. "Now, prove you are worthy of the truth that I am about to tell you."

The Cursed Tower was testing them. And Olivia knew there was no turning back.

Chapter 9

The Shadow King's Army

Olivia held the book tighter as she stepped forward to the boundary of the Hidden Village. The golden light of the village lanterns dimmed behind her. She was alone now, standing at the edge of this place, with only the book in her hands and a map.

The sun went down in the sky, and because of this, it was getting dark. The sky was a mix of purple and blue. A big fog settled on the ground, and a frog hopped around her feet as she walked. She felt like each step was harder than the one she took before. She felt like the air was also trying to slow her down.

Olivia opened her map. As soon as she took it out, she started tracing her finger along the parchment.

She had already read enough stories to understand that time was not always on the hero's side.

A low, ancient sound came through the air. It had rhythm in it; it was like the beating of a giant heart. No, not a heart. Footsteps. Many of them.

Olivia's breath caught for a second.

A massive army advanced across the plains, moving in perfect formation. Hundreds or maybe thousands of soldiers, dressed in black steel armor, marched without hesitation. Their helmets covered their faces, but Olivia could feel the emptiness in her breath. They weren't just soldiers. They were something worse than that.

Shadow was wrapped around the soldiers, and they were moving in a strange way. They were moving too smoothly, too perfectly, as if something was guiding them. Their swords gave a ghostly vibe. In the middle, there was a tall figure sitting on a horse.

And then she realized that he was The Shadow King's General.

Olivia heard stories about him in the village. She also heard some rumors of a warrior who gave up his soul for power. His armor was very different and strong from the others; it was sharp and covered in a silver design. He was wearing a long robe.

She had to find another way to cross the plains.

She looked at her surroundings. She was searching for a route from which she could escape. To her left, there was a dried-out riverbed cutting through the landscape. To her right, a lot of ruined buildings.

Neither one was safe.

But staying there was even worse.

Olivia took a deep breath and made her decision.

She decided that she would go to the riverbed side.

She waited for the perfect moment. For a moment, the army couldn't see her clearly. The soldiers stopped once, and they started moving in a strange way.

Without thinking a single thing, she ran toward the riverbed. The ground was rough and broken. She slipped once, but she went on. Her heartbeat was so loud that she could hear nothing else.

Had they seen her?

Silence.

Then

A sharp voice echoed.

"Did you think we wouldn't find you, storyteller?"

Olivia stopped.

Slowly, she turned her head back.

She was different from everyone else, as standing at the edge of the riverbed was a really big thing. The soldier was tall; his armor was covered in dark silver strings. His eyes were glowing like tiny stones. He had a sword in his hand.

She had been found.

The soldier smiled and tilted his head toward her. He said, "The King has been waiting for you." His voice was deep. "You shouldn't have come here."

Olivia couldn't fight with him as she had no weapons, no armor, nothing but a book in her hands. But she had something else.

She had the story.

"What if I say no?" she asked.

The soldier's smile grew. "Then I will force you to go."

He raised his voice.

Olivia didn't think that this would happen.

She ran down the riverbed. She needed to get out as she had no other option. She needed to find the next chapter in this story before the soldiers took her away.

The soldier kept on chasing her.

Olivia could hear his footsteps; they were too fast and were getting closer. She looked over her shoulder and saw him disappear.

A shadow flickered in front of her.

She barely had time to think of anything else, but before she could think, he appeared again, blocking her path.

The soldier showed his sword again, and this time, she knew she wouldn't be fast enough to let the sword go.

But then a voice came through the air.

"Enough."

The soldier hesitated.

Olivia turned

At the edge of the riverbed, there was another figure, a woman dressed in a deep violet dress. Her hair was flowing in the wind, and her eyes were sharp and knowing.

The soldier kept his sword down and said, "My lady," putting his head down.

"I know," the woman said softly.

Olivia thought, "Who was she? Was she a friend or foe?"

The woman again started looking at Olivia.

She said, "You hold the Book of Lost Names and that means your story is not yet finished."

"Who are you?" she asked.

The woman smiled.

She said, "I am a historian." "And if you want to survive the Shadow King's army, you have to follow me."

Olivia hesitated.

Olivia didn't trust her, but she also didn't have a choice.

With one last look at the soldier, she nodded and said, "Okay."

And with that, she stepped into the unknown once more.

Chapter 10

The Hidden Historian

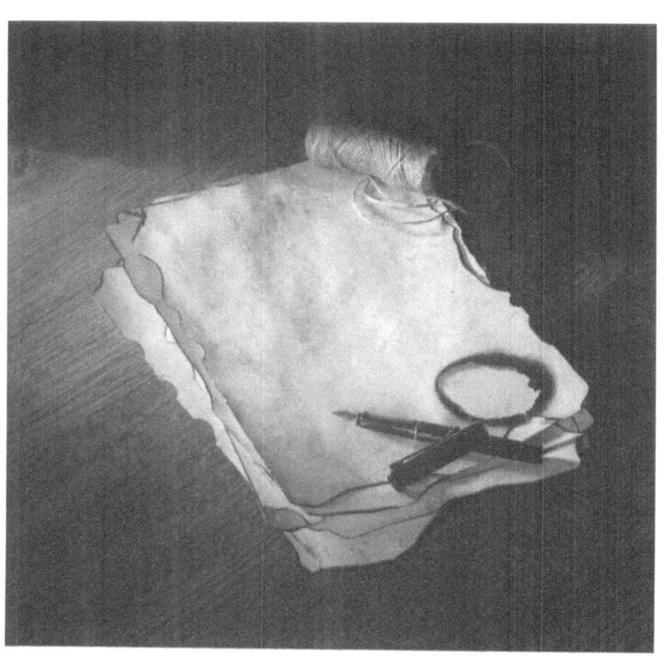

Olivia's heart was beating faster with every second as she followed a mysterious woman along the dry riverbed. The only sounds that could be heard were the balanced rhythm of their footsteps on the ground.

She was filled with questions.

Who was this woman?

Why had the Shadow King's soldier obeyed her?

And the most important question is, could she be trusted?

The woman quickly walked. She was moving so fast that it felt like she had traveled this path a lot of times as she was easily stepping on the sharp rocks.

Finally, Olivia couldn't hold it in any longer.

"Who are you?" she asked; her voice was barely audible.

The woman didn't stop walking. "I told you—I am a historian."

Olivia questioned. "That's not an answer."

Then the woman turned her face for the first time; her dark eyes scared all of them. "And still, is this the only question that you want to answer?"

Olivia said she didn't like puzzles.

They continued walking. The further they traveled, the darker the area became. There were no clouds in the sky.

Then Olivia saw it.

A huge stone entry in front of the wall was half buried in the dirt. Weird symbols were carved on it.

Something about this place felt... different.

"Come," the woman said. "We do not have time to waste."

Olivia took a deep breath and stepped forward. As she passed the entry door, she got a strange feeling. She felt like she was walking through an invisible curtain. The air got warmer and warmer.

They went to a secret valley, fresh and untouched. This valley had tall trees; their leaves were shining as if they were covered in gold. A small stream was flowing gently through the valley, its water sparkling.

This was so different that it felt like they had stepped into an entirely different world.

Olivia turned toward the women and asked, "Where... What is this place?"

The woman smiled and said, "This is a sanctuary. A place that people forgot as time passed, and this place is hidden from the Shadow King."

She asked, "But... how?"

The woman pointed toward the glowing flowers. "Magic. Old magic."

Olivia kept on looking at the flowers. She had read about ancient magic, which was protected by spells that were so strong that not even the most powerful sorcerers could break them.

Was she inside one of those stories now?

Before she could ask another question, the woman turned and started to walk again.

"Come," she said. "There is someone you must meet."

Olivia felt a little nervous, but she followed the women.

The path took them deeper into the valley. At the center of the valley, there was a massive tree—larger than any Olivia had ever seen before.

The woman approached the door and knocked once.

For a moment, there was silence. Then the door opened.

A figure was standing in the doorway.

An old man came; his long beard was silver. His eyes were sharp and bright.

He said, "So," his voice was deep. "The storyteller has finally arrived."

The old man was expecting her to come.

The woman stepped aside and allowed Olivia to enter first. Inside the area, the cottage was warm and filled with the fragrance of old ink and burning wood. A large wooden table was kept in the center of the room; it was covered in maps, ink bottles, and quills.

The old man asked Olivia to sit.

The woman sat beside her, and the old man sat in a large chair that was kept beside the fireplace.

He said, "You are holding something powerful," he said, nodding toward the book in her hands. "Do you understand what it is?"

Olivia said, "I... I know it's special."

The old man said, "Special is a weak word for what you carry."

He came forward; his eyes were dark. "That book contains unfinished stories—stories that were never meant to be forgotten."

Olivia was getting nervous, but she said, "I know."

The old man's gaze sharpened. "Do you?"

He took one of the books from his shelf. He took out a leather-bound book and placed it in front of her. The cover was faded, but the title was still visible:

The Tale of the Shadow King.

Olivia said, "The Shadow King's story... it was in here?"

She looked at the book. The moment she touched it, a strange thing happened; she felt like the book was alive.

She quickly pulled her hand back.

The old man nodded. "That is the story you must finish."

Olivia's eyes widened. "What?"

The woman said, "The Shadow King was not always a villain."

Olivia said, "That's not what the stories say."

The woman said, "The stories were written by those who feared him, but the truth... the truth was lost."

Olivia said, "You're saying the book can... change his story?"

"Not change," the old man corrected her. "Finish."

The weight of the book suddenly felt heavier.

If she could finish the Shadow King's story, could she stop him?

The old man leaned back in his chair. "The choice is yours, storyteller. But choose wisely. Once you write, the story becomes real and it cannot be changed."

Her journey had only just begun.

Chapter 11

The Truth in the Pages

Olivia sat in the historian's cottage and started staring at the old book in front of her. The candlelight flickered. The golden letters on the book were glowing; it felt like they were alive.

The Tale of the Shadow King.

"You're saying... that this book has the true story of the Shadow King?"

The old historian nodded and said, "Yes. And you are the one who must finish it."

Olivia looked down at the book that she had discovered in the library.

"Why me?' she asked. 'Why am I the one who has to do this?"

The old woman answered, "Because you are the only one who can."

Olivia said, "That doesn't make sense. Anyone could pick up a pen and start writing."

The historian smiled, shaking her head. "Not just anyone."

He tapped the book in her hands.

She said, "The library chose you,"

Olivia thought, "Could that be true?"

The underground library called her, but she never thought about why the library would call her. She had assumed it was a coincidence.

But... what if it wasn't?

The historian turned toward the bookshelf behind him and took another book. It was much thicker than the others; it was wrapped in dark green fabric. He placed it in front of her and opened it to a single blank page.

"You must begin here," he said.

Olivia said, "Do you want me to write the Shadow King's story?"

The woman said, "You must finish it." "Only by completing his story can you uncover the truth."

A hundred questions came to her mind.

What if she failed?

What if she made a mistake?

He said, "This ink," "is unlike any other ink. It does not simply record words."

Olivia looked at him. She was confused and asked, "What does it do?"

The woman answered, "It writes... destiny."

The historian said, "Once a story is written with this ink, it becomes real,"

Olivia said, "You mean... whatever I write in this book will actually happen?"

The historian nodded. "Yes."

She wasn't just writing a story.

She was shaping reality.

Olivia looked again at the book. The blank page seemed to glow, as if it were also waiting for her decision.

She could feel the pressure of time.

The Shadow King was growing stronger and stronger day by day.

If she didn't finish this story... the world might be lost.

She took a deep breath and picked up the quill.

And then, she began to write.

Chapter 12

The Maze of Time

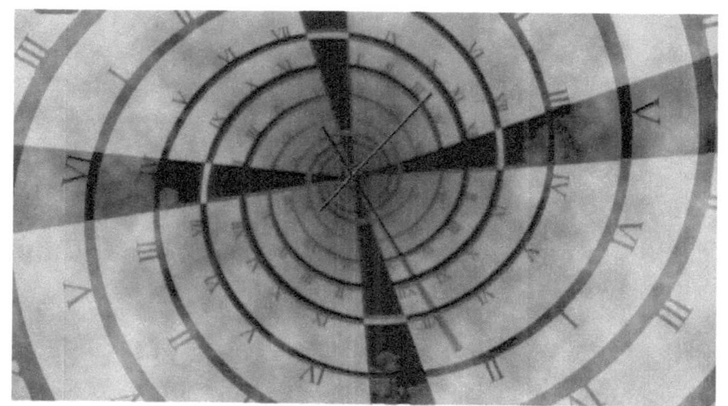

Olivia started staring at the endless maze around her. But the walls were not just made up of stone; they were made of stories.

As she went closer, she saw pictures moving inside the bricks. She saw a picture of a boy holding a book too tightly and his face full of fear. She also saw a girl standing alone in an area, her hands shaking as she tried to decide.

All of them were trapped.

Is this what happens when a story is never finished? When someone is lost inside their own tale?

"You shouldn't be here," a deep voice came through the maze.

The Shadow King stepped. His eyes were gray and unreadable. But this time, he didn't look like a villain.

His expressions were tired.

Olivia said, "You, who are you really?"

The Shadow King touched the stone wall. A soft golden light spread all over.

The books were glowing softly as his fingers touched them. His face looked as if he was wondering about something until he reached for a special book. The same book Olivia had found.

The moment he opened it, the words spilled out like ink, wrapping around his fingers.

The sense changed. Now, he is older than before. He was trapped within the stories.

"You..." She turned her face toward him. "You were the first."

The Shadow King's expression didn't change. "I was the first person to write in the Library of Forgotten Stories," "I was the first to be chosen."

"But... why? Why didn't you finish your story?"

The Shadow King said, "Because I was afraid." Olivia asked, "Afraid of what?" he said. "Afraid of letting go."

His voice lowered. He said, "I kept rewriting. Kept searching for the perfect ending. And before I realized it, 'I became a part of it'."

Will this happen to her as well?

Would she become another forgotten writer who would be lost in an endless story?

"No," she whispered to herself. "That will never happen to me."

The Shadow King said, "Are you sure?"

A deep and empty voice echoed through the air. *"One who enters must finish what they begin."*

The paths she had walked moments ago had disappeared.

She was trapped.

And the only way out of this trap was to finish the story.

Olivia turned. Shadows were flickering.

A shadowy figure grabbed her, but the shadowy figure that had grabbed her had no face. It whispered, "Help me."

Olivia tried to walk backward. "I—I can't!"

"Finish my story."

More hands came. More voices. More unfinished tales.

"Find my ending."

"Give me a name."

"Don't leave me here!"

She turned and ran.

But the voices still followed her.

She realized. *"They're all stuck," "They never finished their stories... and now they can't leave."*

Would she become one of them?

"I have to find the way out."

But there was no exit. No doors and no windows.

The only thing that she had was the book in her hands.

She started by opening every page. The ink shimmered. The words lifted up. And then, new sentences began to write themselves.

And then—

A new path appeared before her.

Not a regular stone path

A bridge of golden light.

Olivia took a deep breath and stepped forward.

The moment her foot touched the bridge, the maze shattered.

The Bridge Between Stories

The maze of stone and smog fell apart. For a moment, she felt like she was floating in an empty space, surrounded by glowing pieces of unfinished stories.

Then her feet touched solid ground.

She was somewhere new.

The golden bridge beneath her feet stretched wide.

The bridge ahead of her extended.

Behind her, there was nothing. The maze was gone.

But there was only one way forward.

She told herself, "Never give up. *Keep moving,*"

Taking a deep breath, she stepped forward.

The moment her foot touched the bridge—

It changed.

A golden light flickered, and suddenly, the bridge wasn't just a bridge anymore.

It was a story.

It was flickering like memories caught between the pages of a book.

She saw a little girl sitting on the steps of an old library; her nose was not buried in a book because it was too big for her hands.

She saw a boy standing in front of a locked door, his fingers holding the handle, and he was afraid to enter.

She saw a young woman standing at a crossroads, and she was staring at a blank page. She was unsure of what to do next.

Each of them felt... familiar.

"Wait — are these —"

Her stories.

All the things that she saw surrounded her, whispering and waiting.

And at the end of the bridge, she saw herself.

She did not see herself as she was now but how she could be in the future.

She saw herself older and wiser, a girl who had faced every fear, every unfinished sentence, and had written her own ending.

A soft voice echoed through the air.

"To walk forward, you must face what you have left behind."

A figure was placed in the center of the bridge.

That figure was tall, wrapped in flowers, and its face was hidden by the light of the bridge. In her hands, she held a quill made of stardust.

Olivia asked, "Who are you?"

The woman answered, "I am the Guardian of this Bridge," she said. "I watch over the stories that still have to be written."

Olivia asked, "And what happens if I keep walking?"

The Guardian said, "That depends." "Will you finish what you started?"

She looked back at the flickering memories of the unfinished stories.

Some were based on adventures.

Some were based on fragments of dreams.

Some were moments that she had been too afraid to complete.

All of them were waiting for her.

Olivia asked, "What if I don't know how they end?"

The Guardian smiled softly.

"Then it's time to find out."

"Every writer must choose: what do they want at the end of their story?"

The Guardian gave Olivia the quills of stardust.

She said, "If you take this, you will have the power to finish any story you start. But be warned, once a story is written, it cannot be unwritten."

"A story that cannot be undone?"

While she was writing her story, she thought of the Shadow King and how he got trapped just because he did not finish his book.

She thought of the voices in the maze, begging for an ending.

She thought of herself.

All the times she had stopped halfway. All the times she had doubted her own words, but no more.

Olivia took the quill. The unfinished stories danced around her, moving faster and faster. Words filled the pages, characters took shapes, and endings came to life.

Olivia said to herself, "There was no turning back."

The Guardian of the Bridge smiled.

"You have chosen well."

Olivia's grip tightened on the quill.

The golden bridge shimmered one last time.

Olivia noticed something new beyond it. A library unlike any she had ever seen before. Not a Library of Forgotten Stories.

But a Library of Endings.

She took a deep breath.

And stepped forward.

Chapter 14

The Library of Endings

The moment she stepped in, she noticed that the golden light disappeared, and something more shocking than that was that she found herself on a huge shelf of books.

Unlike the Library of Forgotten Stories, this was something different; this time, the books did not speak; they were still.

Each shelf was perfectly arranged, and all the books were lined up neatly. It was very clean. There was no dust, no missing pages, and no faded ink. Every book in this library was complete.

Some of the titles were:

- *The Star Weaver's Last Wish*
- *A Kingdom Beneath the Waves*
- *The Tale of the Wandering Prince*

Every single one had an ending.

For a moment, she felt strange because the place was very quiet and peaceful.

But then, a thought came into her mind.

"If this is the Library of Endings... does that mean that every story here has already been told and has already been ended?"

In the middle of the room, there was a really big statue carved from white marble. And on top of it, there was a single book.

This book was not an ordinary book. This book was different. Unlike the others, this book was unfinished.

Olivia took a cautious step forward toward the book.

The book's cover was smooth and glowing.

But when she touched it, the title appeared.

The title read, "The Story of Olivia."

Her heart stopped for a moment.

Olivia's hands were shaking as she opened the book.

She flipped page after page and saw her own life written with ink.

She stepped into the library for the first time.

The day she learned to write her own stories.

The moment she discovered the hidden staircase beneath the library.

Her journey through the world of forgotten stories.

Her battle against the Shadow King.

Her choice to take the quill.

Everything she had done was here.

But as she reached the last written page

It ended.

The final words were:

"And then, she stepped into the Library of Endings... and—"

The rest of the page was blank.

"My story is unfinished."

She looked at the quill in her hand. The Guardian's words echoed in her mind.

"Once a story is written, it cannot be unwritten."

Did this mean... she had the power to write her own ending?

What kind of ending did she want?

Did she want to go home—to return to her world, leaving this magical place behind?

Did she want to stay—becoming the next Keeper of Stories?

Did she want to start a new adventure beyond the library and into the unknown?

The possibilities were swirling around her mind.

For the first time, no one could decide for her.

This time, she was the author.

Olivia stared at the blank page.

She had spent so much time finishing other people's stories.

Now, she had to finish her own.

A familiar voice came.

"You've come far, Olivia."

"You knew this would happen," Olivia said slowly.

The Keeper nodded. "From the moment you opened that first book, your story began to change."

Olivia asked, "But... how do I know what to write?"

The Keeper smiled.

"This is entirely up to you."

He gives Olivia a key.

He said, "This is for you," and he placed it gently into her palm.

Olivia stared at it. "What does it open?"

The Keeper said, "A new beginning."

Before she could ask what he meant—

The library around her began to fade.

The bookshelves dissolved into the golden mist.

Would she be back in her town's library, as if nothing had happened?

Would she enter a new world, one she had yet to write?

Would she return as the next Keeper, forever guiding unfinished stories?

The Golden Quill glowed.

Slowly, she took the quill and opened the last page.

And she wrote.

"Olivia took a deep breath, knowing that wherever this door led, she was ready."

She turned the handle.

The door swung open.

And she stepped through.

Chapter 15

The Other Side of the Door

Olivia stepped through the door.

For a moment, there was nothing.

No floor beneath her feet.

No sky above her head.

No sound, no light – just emptiness.

Then, everything shifted.

And then she landed.

Olivia's eyes finally opened.

She was not in the library.

She was in a wide and open field.

She turned in a slow circle.

From the distance, she saw a city that was very different, and she had never seen a city like that before. Bridges connected the buildings, and everywhere, people were walking through the streets.

It was a city of stories.

Olivia asked, "Where am I?"

"Welcome to the City of Unwritten Tales."

There was a boy standing behind her, with messy brown hair and bright green eyes. He carried a satchel filled with ink bottles and quills.

"Who are you?" she asked.

The boy said, "The real question is— who are you?"

Olivia frowned. "I'm Olivia. And I—"

She hesitated.

She didn't know how to finish that sentence.

Before, she was a reader who loved books.

But then, she became a story traveler who stepped into unfinished tales.

Then, she had been a warrior who fought against the Shadow King.

And now she is someone new.

The boy asked her, "You don't have an ending yet, do you?"

Olivia slowly shook her head and said, "Yes."

He said, "Good," "That means you belong here."

The boy gave the girl a tour of the city.

Some people sat in cafes, scribbling in notebooks.

Others gathered in groups and were spinning stories aloud.

A few held blank books and were waiting for their covers to be filled.

Olivia said: *"This place... it's alive."*

The boy nodded in agreement.

Olivia asked, "And what happens when someone finishes writing their story?"

"Then they have to choose," he said quietly.

"Choose what?"

"Whether they leave... or stay forever."

She looked at her own book—the one she started writing in the Library of Endings.

It was still unfinished.

And now, she had to decide whether she would stay in the City of Unwritten Tales and keep writing.

Or was it time to go home?

The boy sat beside her and he was watching her carefully. "You're thinking about going back, aren't you?"

She nodded. "But... I don't know how."

The boy said, "That's easy. You write it."

Olivia asked, "What?"

He said, "You have the Golden Quill. It doesn't just write stories; it writes reality. If you write that you're going home, the story will make it happen."

"I feel that's... that's too much power for one person."

The boy answered, "Every writer has power. Every time you tell a story, you shape the world. You decide what happens next. That's why words are the most powerful magic here."

Olivia stared at the quill in her hand.

If she wrote the words *"Olivia found herself back in her library,"* would it really happen?

Did she want it to happen?

Her journey started in a quiet library in her town.

She faced dangers, solved mysteries, and became part of stories bigger than herself.

And now, she had the power to decide what happened next.

Olivia asked, "What would be the best choice?"

The boy smiled. "Whatever you choose, Olivia, it will be the right story. Because it's yours."

Olivia took a deep breath and began to write.

Chapter 16

The Story That Writes Itself

The page in front of her was blank, and it was waiting for her decision.

She had two choices.

Option One: She could write that she wants to go back home. Back to the old library, back to her normal life, and back to a world where only stories existed, not these unfinished tales.

Option Two: She could stay here, explore, write, and live inside stories forever.

"Do you want to know a secret?" the boy beside her asked.

Olivia turned toward him. "A secret about what?"

He pointed at her book. "About how this really works."

The boy smiled. "A story is not about what you just write; it is something you live. The moment you pick up that quill, your choices will start shaping the world around you. Your decision is not just about the words on a page; it's about what you truly want."

Olivia asked, "But what if I make the wrong choice?"

The boy answered, "There are no wrong choices in a story. There are only new choices, not wrong choices."

Her mind went back to everything she had been through: the moment she first found the hidden door, the underground library, the battle against the Shadow King, the stories she had completed, the people she had met.

Everything had led her here.

Suddenly, Olivia realized something. She didn't have to choose just one path.

She could write her own path.

Olivia took a deep breath and began to write.

The moment the quill's tip touched the page, the page shimmered.

The boy said, "That's it. You've figured it out."

Olivia asked, "Figured out what?"

He said, "You're not just a person who travels. That means you don't have to stay or leave; you can move between worlds whenever you want."

She asked, "Can I?"

He nodded and said, "Yes. The library, the kingdom, this city… they're all connected. Every book, every unfinished story, is a doorway and you hold the key to that doorway."

This means that she could go home when she wanted — but also return to the world of stories whenever she needed to.

She didn't have to leave the books behind.

She can live in them.

The words on the page rearranged themselves, creating a new title:

"The Story Weaver's Journey."

The boy smiled. "Looks like your next chapter is about to begin."

Olivia grabs the handle; she gets very excited.

She wasn't just a reader anymore.

She was a storyteller.

And her story was far from over.

Chapter 17

The Return Home

Olivia took a deep breath and turned the handle of the door.

As soon as she opened the door, she felt like no ground was beneath her.

She was falling.

Wind rushed through her, and the fragrance of old books filled her nose.

Thud!

Olivia landed on something soft: a pile of cushions. She opened her eyes and found herself back in the underground library.

The chandeliers that were above flickered gently. The air smelled of ink and parchment, mixed with something magical.

She sat quickly, and her hands were shaking as she touched the hardcover book that was kept close to her. The title read: The Story Weaver's Journey. The book was closed; its golden letters were glowing.

Was all of this real?

She looked around. She was still expecting the Shadow King's army to come or the people from Eldoria to call her name. But everything was silent.

The only sound she could hear was people flipping pages.

Then, a soft cough.

"Olivia."

The Keeper said, "You did well, child." "You helped finish a story that had been waiting for its ending."

Olivia touched the book beside her. "Was it all real?"

The Keeper smiled. "What do you think?"

"I think... it was real," she said finally.

The Keeper nodded. "Then it was."

Olivia looked up at the shelves of unfinished stories. The books seemed alive; their pages were moving as if they were whispering to each other.

"Are there... more?" she asked.

The Keeper answered, "Thousands or maybe millions. Each one is waiting for a storyteller like you to help them find their ending."

Olivia had a lot of questions, such as, "More adventures? More stories to save? More doors to open?"

She said, "Then I guess I'm not done yet."

The Keeper said, "No, Olivia. Your journey has only just begun."

Suddenly, the lanterns grew brighter, the books spoke softly, and something shifted the air as if the entire library had been waiting for this moment.

Olivia stepped forward. She reached out and traced the untold stories.

Then, her hand paused on a new book.

Its cover was deep blue, with silver keys on top.

She turned to the Keeper and asked, "What is this one about?"

He gave her a glowing smile. "There is only one way to find out."

Olivia took a deep breath and opened the book.

The golden light came again.

And just before the light took her away, she heard the Keeper say:

"Welcome back, Story Weaver."

About the Author

Vagisha and Her First Book: *The Hidden Literature*

Vagisha is a 12-year-old girl. She wanted to write her very first book. She had always loved reading, getting lost in magical worlds, and imagining new adventures. But this time, she wasn't just a reader; she was going to be a writer!

She thought for days about what her book should be about. Then, an idea sparked in her mind—a story about an underground library filled with unfinished books. These books held forgotten dreams and abandoned stories. When someone read them, they were transported inside and had to help the characters find their ending. Vagisha named her book *The Hidden Literature.*

Excited, she grabbed her notebook and started writing. At first, the words flowed easily. She wrote about a brave girl named Olivia, who found the secret library and got pulled into different stories. But soon, Vagisha realized writing a book wasn't as simple as she thought. She sometimes got stuck, unsure of what should happen next.

But Vagisha didn't give up. She set a goal to write a little every day. She made a list of all the characters, their adventures, and how each story should end.

After hard work, she finally finished *The Hidden Literature*. Holding her story in her hands, Vagisha felt proud. She had turned her idea into something real. Now, she wasn't just a dreamer she was a writer, ready to share her stories with the world!

www.ingramcontent.com/pod-product-compliance
Lightning Source LLC
Chambersburg PA
CBHW020641160726
47991CB00003B/975